Charles E. Martin

Greenwillow Books, New York

Watercolors and ink were used for the full-color
illustrations. The display type was hand lettered
by the artist. The text type is Goudy Old Style.

Library of Congress Cataloging in Publication Data
Martin, Charles E., (date)   For rent.
Summary: After renting their clubhouse to summer
tourists, the children on an island find that
being landlords is harder than they thought.
1. Children's stories, American.
[1. Landlord and tenant—Fiction.
2. Islands—Fiction.
3. Tourist trade—Fiction]   I. Title.
PZ7.M356777Fo 1985   [E]   85-864
ISBN 0-688-05716-0
ISBN 0-688-05717-9 (lib. bdg.)

FOR FLORENCE

It was the last day of school. Mrs. Gray held a letter in her hand. It was from Mrs. Burton, a lady who had grown up on the island and had recently moved away. It was addressed to the island children. It said:

When I was a little girl, my family gave me the small shed on the cove. My friends and I spent a lot of time there. It was our clubhouse and our second home. Now I want you to have it. Clean it up, take good care of it, and be as happy with it as we were.

The children were very quiet. They had all liked Mrs. Burton, but they had never expected anything like this.

"It's a wonderful present," Mrs. Gray said. "Let's all go look at it."

"We can paint it," Heather said. Everyone agreed that it should be bright red.

Their parents said there was plenty of paint in the fishhouses for them to use. "We'll help when we can," said Sam's father, "but you will have to do most of the work yourselves." They started working on the shed the next day.

They worked on it as hard and as often as they could. Sam's father came and checked it for leaks. One day Heather's mother said it looked spiffy. "Why don't you rent it?" she said. "You could rent a parrot cage on this island in the summer."

Everyone agreed it was a good idea. They would rent the shed in the summer and use it as a clubhouse in the winter. They put up "For Rent" signs on the boat and on the dock.

A man phoned Heather's house. He wanted the shed for the first two weeks in July. He said he was a writer and that he needed a quiet place to work. When the boat came in, they all knew that the tall man with the typewriter was their tenant. They walked him to the shed. He liked it very much. He said if he needed anything he would tell them.

He was never at home when they went to see him. Once Kate saw him from her father's boat, walking on the headland. At the end of the week he came to Heather's house and said he had to leave the island. He had won a poetry prize and had to attend the ceremony. At the shed they found everything in order. Sam's mother told them there was a couple who wanted the shed and could be there in two days.

They met Mr. and Mrs. Dumpson at the dock. When Mrs. Dumpson saw the shed, she said it was darling, but a little small. A black cat appeared at the open door.

"Whose cat is that?" asked Mrs. Dumpson.

"Oh, that's Polly," Kate said. "She belongs to everyone."

"You will have to remove her," Mrs. Dumpson said. "We do not like stray cats."

Sam took Polly to Fish Beach and left her there with two of her friends and lots of sea gulls.

The next day Sam, Jonathan, and Mae visited the Dumpsons to see if all was well. "It's the foghorn," Mrs. Dumpson said. "Why does it have to be so loud? Mr. Dumpson can't play his cello and he has to practice every day." The foghorn continued to sound all that day and night.

The following day was clear and hot. Mr. Dumpson appeared at Heather's door. "There's no water," he said. "I'm hot and I need a shower."

"The water will be running again by noon," Heather told him. "The pipes are being fixed. There's a notice up at the store. But you can use your well. It's been tested and it's perfect."

Mr. Dumpson said he preferred to wait until noon. It was a hot walk back to the cottage. "That's it," said Mr. Dumpson. "My mind is made up."

On Sunday the Dumpsons told Sam they were sorry, but islands were not for them. They would be leaving Wednesday, on the early boat.

"Being landlords is harder than I thought it would be," said Sam. "Maybe we should stop."

But Kate's mother had heard of a lady who was eager to rent a place, anyplace, for the rest of the summer. She said that not all people were alike and that they shouldn't give up so quickly. They all went to meet Eve Birdle at the dock.

Miss Birdle seemed very happy to be there. They worried about getting all her things into the small shed. "Everything's fine," she said. "I can always find a place to put things." When they left, they saw that she and Polly were getting along very well together.

Miss Birdle got right down to work. They would see her before breakfast, carrying her gear along the road. They watched her paint all over the island—on Fish Beach, Lighthouse Hill, the ice pond, and the dock. She liked it when they asked her questions.

One Saturday she invited all of them to go out painting with her
on the headlands, facing out to sea. She said she would bring paints,
crayons, colored pencils, and paper. They said they would bring
lunch. As they worked, Miss Birdle talked about light and shadow,
and how to get the colors they wanted. They all worked hard on
their drawings.

Summer was almost over. Miss Birdle invited them to the shed for ice cream and cake. They asked about her paintings. She was sorry, she said, but they were all packed.

The next day they said goodbye to her at the dock. She said she would keep in touch, and if they rented the shed again next summer, perhaps they would keep her in mind as a tenant.

School opened soon after. Mrs. Gray said that their generous contribution to the Activity Fund from their rent money would make it possible for them to go to Washington, D.C. for their annual trip. With two of the mothers along, they traveled by boat, train, and bus. They stayed in a motel near the White House. They saw everything: the Capitol, the Senate in action, the museums, the Library of Congress.

But best of all, Mrs. Gray had a surprise for them. They were guests of honor at the opening of an exhibition of paintings—by Miss Eve Birdle.